THE
GOLDEN
COCKEREL

THE GOLDEN COCKEREL

AND OTHER FAIRY TALES

by
ALEKSANDR PUSHKIN
TRANSLATED FROM THE FRENCH BY JESSIE WOOD

ILLUSTRATED BY BORIS ZVORYKIN

INTRODUCTION BY RUDOLF NUREYEV

DOUBLEDAY

NEW YORK   LONDON   TORONTO   SYDNEY   AUCKLAND

PUBLISHED BY DOUBLEDAY
a division of Bantam Doubleday Dell
Publishing Group, Inc., 666 Fifth Avenue, New York, New York 10103

DOUBLEDAY and the portrayal of an anchor with a dolphin are
trademarks of Doubleday, a division of
Bantam Doubleday Dell Publishing Group, Inc.

Library of Congress Cataloging-in-Publication Data

Pushkin, Aleksandr Sergeevich, 1799–1837.
  [Fairy tales. English. Selections]
  The golden cockerel and other fairy tales / by Aleksandr Pushkin;
illustrated by Boris Zvorykin; translated from the French by Jessie Wood;
introduction by Rudolf Nureyev.—1st ed.
      p. cm.
  "Originally published in France as Le coq d'or in 1925 by H. Piazza"—T.p. verso.
  Contents: The golden cockerel—The Tsar Saltan—The dead princess—The
fisherman and the fish.
  1. Fairy tales—Russian S.F.S.R.—Translations into English. [1. Fairy tales.]
I. Zvorykin, Boris Vassilievich, b. 1872, ill.
II. Wood, Jessie. III. Title.
PG3343.S513 1989
891.73'3—dc19
[Fic]   89–1320
                                                                   CIP
                                                                    AC
ISBN 0-385-26252-3

Originally published in France as *Le Coq d'Or* in 1925 by H. Piazza

Introduction and English-language translation
copyright © 1989 by Doubleday, a division of Bantam Doubleday Dell Publishing
Group, Inc.

Designed by Michael Mendelsohn of M 'N O Production Services, Inc.

Printed in Italy

October 1990

FIRST EDITION

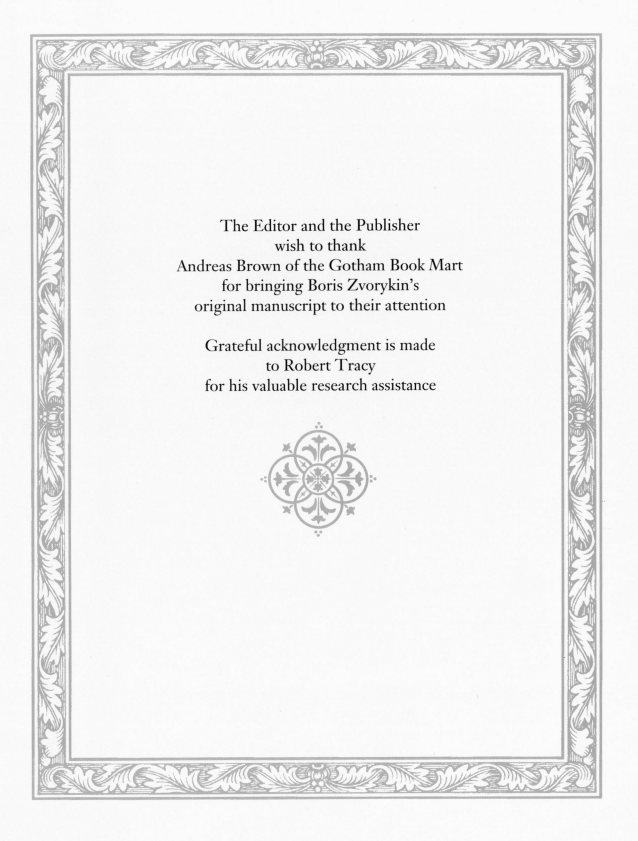

The Editor and the Publisher
wish to thank
Andreas Brown of the Gotham Book Mart
for bringing Boris Zvorykin's
original manuscript to their attention

Grateful acknowledgment is made
to Robert Tracy
for his valuable research assistance

CONTENTS

ABOUT THE ILLUSTRATOR

The illustrations for this book were done by Boris Vassi-lievich Zvorykin, a member of the Slavic Revival move-ment in Russia. Born in Moscow in 1872, he graduated from the Moscow Academy of Painting, then devoted himself to decorative art, especially book illustrations. He painted the murals for the old Cathedral at Simferopol and received other important commissions from the Imperial Court: a book celebrating the tercentenary of the House of Romanov, a magnificent volume on the Theo-dorovsky Cathedral at Tsarskoe Selo, and an illuminated manuscript twenty meters long, commemorating the rees-tablishment of the Patriarchal Throne in Russia. For twenty years he was art director of the publishing house A. A. Levenson, pioneers of *éditions de luxe* in Russia. He created books in the style of illuminated manuscripts, and his reputation grew to rival that of Ivan Bilibin, Russia's greatest illustrator. Zvorykin left Russia after the Revolu-tion and made his way to Paris, where he found a job in the publishing house of H. Piazza. There, in exile, he continued to illustrate Russian fairy tales.

INTRODUCTION

The four tales in this book illuminate different aspects of Russian art, of the Russian soul. Derived from folktales told by peasants from time immemorial, they are the oldest voice of Mother Russia. They were recorded in this form in the nineteeenth century by Pushkin, Russia's greatest poet, as told to him by his nanny, Arina Rodionovna. Artists from all fields have always been drawn to Pushkin, and his writing inspired great Russian music and dance in his time. Serge Diaghilev, the impresario who brought the Ballets Russes to the West, based some of his productions on Pushkin's work. For all, Pushkin endures as the Romantic Hero.

Aleksandr Sergeyevich Pushkin was the freedom inspirer of Russia. His great poems, "Volnost" (Ode to Liberty) and "Derevnya" (The Village), urged people to raise their heads and change the times. He was responsible for igniting the best there was in Russian society.

He had read the French writers of the Enlightenment, Diderot and Rousseau. His closest friends were the young Russian officers who had been in Paris with Tsar Alexander I after the defeat of Napoleon and breathed the new ideas of freedom there. They all knew his poems by heart. Everyone did. There was wild enthusiasm for his poetry and for his scathing words against authority, against serfdom. He was the voice of liberty and the literary idol of the day when he was just twenty years old.

In 1820 the Tsar's secret police decided he was too subversive. He was arrested and banished from St. Petersburg to a forsaken province in the south of Russia.

Five years later those officers, his friends, led the unfortunate December uprising against the new Tsar Nicholas I. They were all exiled, sent to Siberia, or beheaded.

When Pushkin reached the south he fell sick. He was befriended by General Rayevski, a hero of the war of 1812, who took pity on him and invited him to convalesce on a family journey to the Caucasus and the Crimea. Rayevski's daughter Marya would become Pushkin's ideal woman. For she would marry one of the Decembrist officers, Prince Volkonsky, in an arranged marriage, and though she did not love the Prince, she would join him in his exile in Siberia for the rest of her life. Marya was the model for Tatyana in *Eugene Onegin*, and Pushkin named his first child after her.

In the south he loved the wild landscape, the Circassian tribes, the strange peoples, and he collected their legends. Because he offended a southern count, he was transferred to the other end of Russia, to his mother's estate of Mikhailovskoe, near Pskov. There he got to know the peasants and wrote down their folktales and their songs. He had gone back to his source, nurse Arina, the person who had loved him most in childhood.

Pushkin's parents, like most aristocratic families then, paid no attention to him. His mother read novels, his father gambled, they went to balls every night, and had a French tutor for their children. His grandmother, a descendant of Abram Hannibal, the Abyssinian general of Peter the Great, was the one who supervised his care. In her household there was a freed serf from her estate, Arina Rodionovna, who became Pushkin's nurse from the day he was born.

She used to tell him bedtime stories of the old folktales, stories passed from age to age. It comforted him that she was still there when he was banished to Mikhailovskoe.

Pushkin was bored to death and isolated in that flat and

dreary province. "God, the sky is gray here and the moon looks like a turnip," he wrote. "Do you know how I spend my time? I write, I eat late, I ride in the evening. I listen to my nanny's tales and fill in the gaps in my wretched education. What wonders they are, her old tales, every one is a poem." Arina appears in *Eugene Onegin* as Tatyana's nurse.

Pushkin had the greatest admiration for Byron. He was actually proud that he had slept with one of Byron's mistresses, Calypso Polichrani, a Greek girl. He made Don Juan lists of women he had slept with and women he had loved platonically.

In *Eugene Onegin* he invented a Russian heel, a tracing paper copy of Childe Harold. At one moment he even had him go and fight somewhere in Albania, which is not very far from Greece, where Byron went to fight for Greek independence—and to die at thirty-six, the same age at which Pushkin died.

Nicholas I let Pushkin return to St. Petersburg after six years in exile, but his secret police still kept him under surveillance. Pushkin wasn't too fond of tsars. He said, "I have seen three tsars in my life. The first ordered me to take off my hat, and as I was too young to be scolded myself, he scolded my nurse instead. The second was hardly an admirer of mine, and although the third has raised me to the exalted rank of gentleman of the bedchamber in my dotage, I have no great desire to change him for a fourth. Let us leave well enough alone."

Back in St. Petersburg Pushkin completed his masterpiece, *Eugene Onegin*. It had taken him ten years. A novel in verse about Russian society, its central character is Onegin, who is bored and tired with life in the English fashion. He wants something better, something more: to go to Europe and follow a path like Childe Harold's. When Onegin returns from his travels after many years, still unsatisfied, he sees Tatyana again and realizes that true happiness was always in the family.

Onegin was a prophecy. The duel in which Onegin kills Lensky foretold Pushkin's own death.

In 1831 Pushkin married Natalya Nikolaevna Goncharova, a beautiful flirt with an empty head, who was bored with his poetry. The Tsar was infatuated with her, would ride his horse under her window. When Pushkin wouldn't let Natalya go to court balls, the Tsar made him a *Camerpage*, a Gentleman of the Bedchamber, so that he was obliged to go and be in attendance on the Tsar. "They say we are going to march in pairs like convent girls," Pushkin wrote. Russia's greatest poet was put into a page boy uniform with a lot of young boys of eighteen. Pushkin saw it as a mockery while the Tsar was sleeping with his wife. He was in a trap.

Natalya would dance till five in the morning, sleep, then have lunch at eight in the evening. Pushkin wrote her letters to restrain her frivolity.

"Don't listen to your sisters, don't drag yourself to all kinds of *goulanghi*, all kinds of clubs, lunches. Don't dance on in balls to the morning. Go to sleep early. Don't let Father see the children because he might frighten them. Don't read lousy books. Don't soil yourself with strange images, fantasies. Coquetry, O.K. I permit. As much as your soul wants. Don't ride on wild horses. If you are not happy with the German nurse, throw her out without ceremony or false pretense."

Pushkin needed to get on with his writing and tried to resign his post, but the Tsar would not release him. Anonymous letters were circulated about Natalya and the Tsar. A Frenchman named D'Anthès, with whom she was also flirting, repeated them. Pushkin was forced to defend his wife's honor in a duel and he was shot. It took him two days to die. When he was dying, he asked for *kissel*, a blackberry syrup. It reminded him of his childhood. People gathered outside his house. The Tsar became fearful and had his coffin taken at night to a monastery. At his funeral the courtiers were amazed at the enormous crowds. They were delighted to be rid of a dangerous liberal. Prince Vyazemsky asked a poor man, "You knew Pushkin?" The man answered, "No, but I am Russian."

So Pushkin was dead, but he left his writings. They inspired some of Russia's greatest music, opera, ballet: *Boris Godunov, The Queen of Spades, The Fountain of Bakchisarai, Ruslan and Ludmilla, The Golden Cockerel.* And he left the incomparable *Eugene Onegin.*

The first chapter of *Onegin* has the best tribute to ballet any writer has ever made. Pushkin was an astute observer like Byron. On one side he wrote the story line; on the other he digressed with flights of fancy in which he observed the political situation, the customs of the country, literature, art, and that is where dance comes into it. How great a thing at that time was dance: Didelot with his choreography, Pushkin's admiration for the dancing of Istomina. For Pushkin the art of dance was not just a technical thing but was inspired by a higher longing.

He writes about his favorite ballerina, Audotia Istomina, in great detail, describes how she made *ronds de jambe.* She was very famous for jumping. He makes one see how she jumps, how she flies away from the mouth of Aeolus. When Istomina was downgraded in 1826, Pushkin attributed it to the vogue for foreign ballerinas and wrote a novel about it, *Two Dancers.* This mania for foreign ballerinas lasted a very long time—until the advent of Matilda Kschessinskaya, who was loved by Nicholas II, the last Tsar.

There was a film made once for a competition of my school, the Kirov, in 1958, I think. We went to Moscow and had a competition, the Kirov Ballet School, the Bolshoi, fifteen schools of the U.S.S.R. And I won the competition. They compiled a film of the best applicants, and they quoted Pushkin in it with these words from *Eugene Onegin:* "From the overflow of soul a dancer flies."

What it means is: Dance has a meaning equal to poetry when it is spiritually inspired. It is not just the technical ability to do steps that is important, but like a motor you must generate the meaning. That is how Pushkin summed up the Romantic movement in dance, where the body defies gravity and tries to reach a higher sphere. It is inspired. Dance is inspired. What you cannot say in words you say in movement.

Pushkin's fairy tales were eagerly taken as subjects for ballets, by Frenchmen of course. They were the most important choreographers at the Maryinski Theater in St. Petersburg. Dance came to Russia from France. French choreographers found a good fertile ground there, and on the great responsive bodies of the dancers they created Russian ballets. First there was Charles-Louis Didelot (1767–1837), whom Pushkin admired. He said his ballets were worth all of French literature. Dance in Russia is greatly indebted to Didelot and to the Russian-French coproductions of Jules Perrot. Then came Saint-Léon, who used Pushkin's "Tale of the Golden Fish." Romantic ballet begins with Filippo Taglioni, father of the great dancer Marie. He created *La Sylphide.* Petipa, who came last, wavered between the romanticism of Perrot and the classicism of Saint-Léon. Petipa spent a major part of his life in Russia and was very much taken with Pushkin, although he didn't read or speak Russian.

He is responsible for creating the Russian ballet that Diaghilev later exported to the West. The last pre-Diaghilev ballet of any note was Delibes's *Coppélia*, written about 1870. Then dance collapsed in Russia from 1880 on. Diaghilev was the one who revived it, liberated it.

Serge Diaghilev, who was from Moscow, had been influenced by the Slavic Revival movement of the 1890s, which started there. Artists went all over the country looking for the folk motifs of old Russia, from architecture, embroidery, icons, jeweled weapons, and they wove them into modern art. When Diaghilev moved to St. Petersburg and started his magazine *Mir Iskusstva* (The

World of Art), he fused Slavic Revival with Art Nouveau and made foreign and native artists pull together to create something that was totally new yet uniquely Russian.

When Diaghilev took the Ballets Russes to Paris in 1909, he electrified the world. No one could believe what they saw. He gave dance another dimension, new ideas, new shapes, new choreography, new stage decoration. What fabulous artists he introduced to the West. For dancers he had Nijinsky, Pavlova, Karsavina; for choreographers, Fokine, Nijinsky, Massine, Balanchine. For music he had Stravinsky, Rimsky-Korsakov, Borodin, Prokofiev. For scenery, Bakst, Benois, Doboujinsky, Roerich, Gontcharova.

It was a kind of Russian patriotism. Russians wanted to leave a strong mark, to show that Russian art existed. They wanted to say to the West, "Look at this, instead of at European art, which is always there."

Diaghilev basically worked with committees: Benois, Bakst, Doboujinsky, Fokine. The committee worked on the story, and everybody contributed. Then they looked for the composer, then for the scenery designer. Bakst died of overwork. They made him do everything. He could never say no.

Diaghilev revered Pushkin. He had a requiem mass said on the anniversary of his death every year. He had taken the great basso Chaliapin to Paris with the opera of Pushkin's *Boris Godunov*. He took Pushkin's "The Golden Cockerel" to Paris as a ballet. He owned the most extraordinary collection of books on Pushkin at the end of his life. Apparently he didn't read them, but just kept them.

The long-lost artist who illustrated Pushkin's fairy tales for this book was Boris Zvorykin, a member of the Slavic Revival movement. He was second fiddle to Ivan Bilibin, the greatest illustrator of fairy tales. Zvorykin's brilliant pictures look like Russian illuminated manuscripts. After the Revolution he lived as a poor emigré in Paris. In exile Zvorykin was homesick for old Russia—so he found work with a French publisher and painted illustrations for Russian fairy tales.

Telling fairy tales in Russia is an old tradition. In America the television set is the center for the family; in Russia it is the samovar. You would sit around it listening to stories, drinking tea, sipping *kissel*. I remember from summer childhood the pestle the witch Baba Yaga flies away on was what we used to bash wheat.

Zvorykin's images put you in a trance. Domes, spires, tents with flags, magic trees with golden nuts, great boyars and princesses wearing *kokoshnik* headdresses, feasts with pomegranates in enameled bowls, evil peacocks. His illustrations made people enjoy his love of folklore and costume. He was fascinated by those things. His wooden architecture, his *isbas*, peasant huts, were painted in bold, rich colors. You leave the image happy. It is sumptuous—but also primitive. From the child's point of view the images were rich and promised good fortune. You think, "Poverty never strikes those people." Zvorykin made poverty luxurious.

I look at his pictures and think, "Why don't I live in fairy-tale times?"

—Rudolf Nureyev
Paris, 1988

18

The four fairy tales written by the great Russian poet Pushkin, presented in this book, are among the most famous tales of the genre in Russian literature.

According to the poet himself, he was inspired by the wonderful stories told him as a child. These tales owe a great deal to the popular poetry of ancient Russia.

The poet's imagination and fantasy have re-created scenes of everyday life in the Russia of days gone by. This is why illustrator Boris Zvorykin has chosen to give this work the intricate and detailed look of an ancient manuscript.

The illustrations have been conceived in the style of sixteenth- and seventeenth-century Russian miniatures. The borders, fleurons, decorated capitals, the titles in calligraphic form with their complicated interlaced design, everything in this work conforms absolutely to the ornamentation of a true Russian Renaissance manuscript.

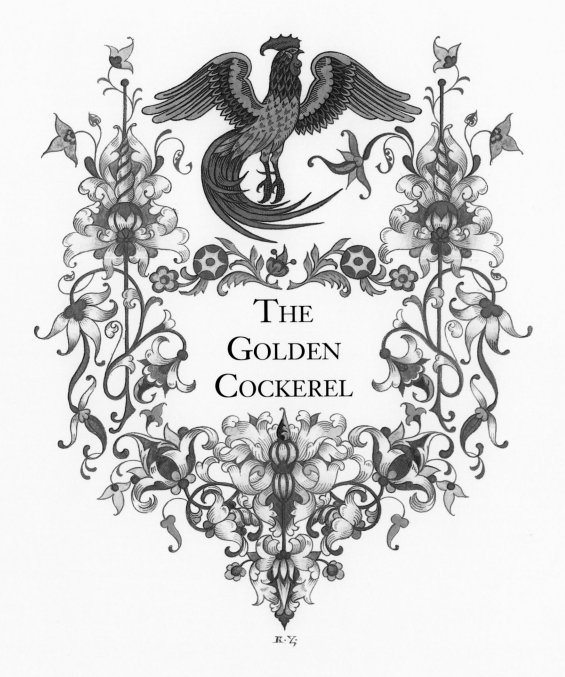

THE
GOLDEN
COCKEREL

THE
GOLDEN COCKEREL

The illustrious Tsar Dadone reigned in a very
isolated country on the far side of the world. He
had spent his entire youth invading the lands of
his enemies. Now that he is old and weary of
feats of arms, he wants to live in peace, but his
neighbors see an opportunity to take their re-
venge. They attack without respite and inflict

great losses on his army. The frontiers of the empire are under constant threat.

Dadone must reinforce his army. Alas, his generals are constantly caught off guard. Whenever they expect the enemy to come from the south, he looms up in the east. Beaten off on one front, a band of attackers materializes on another.

It can't go on like this! The Tsar cried with rage, and tosses and turns all night. At last he sent for a sage; a man who was a eunuch and a great student of astronomy.

The man arrived. He pulled out of his bag a golden cockerel, which he gave to Dadone with these words:

"Place this cockerel on the weather vane atop your highest tower. He will be your most loyal protector. As long as you have nothing to fear, he will not move. But at the slightest threat of war, the slightest menace of invasion, my cockerel will raise his head, cry out in alarm, and turn in the direction of the danger."

The Tsar thanked the eunuch and rewarded him with heaps of gold.

"You have rendered me such a service that I shall grant your most cherished wish as though it were my own."

High atop a tower, the cockerel watches the frontiers of the empire. At the least disturbance, this faithful servitor awakes, flutters his wings, turns toward the peril, and sings:

"Cockadoodledoo! Reign on, and sleep soundly!"

And the warlike neighbors no longer dare to attack the Tsar who inflicted such dreadful defeats upon them in the past.

A year went by, then another and another. The cockerel had not stirred.

One day Dadone was wakened by a loud noise.

"Beloved our Tsar! Father of the people!" one of his generals shouted. "Oh, misfortune! Misfortune!"

"What?" asked Dadone, yawning. "Who is here? What misfortune?"

The general answered:

"The cockerel has crowed! The capital is filled with terror and tumult. . . ."

The Tsar dashed to the window. The cockerel, fluttering in agitation, is facing toward the Orient. There is no time to lose.

"To horse! To horse!"

Dadone's army wends its way forth, led by his eldest son. The cockerel is still. The capital is peaceful. The Tsar quite forgets the recent danger.

Eight days pass without news of the army. Did it do battle or not?

The cockerel has sung once more. The Tsar raises another army. His second son is put in command. He will go to his brother's rescue.

Eight days pass without news of the second army! The city is terrified.

The cockerel has just crowed again! The Tsar raises a third army, over which he personally takes command, even though he has no idea of what he will do.

The regiments march night and day. They are exhausted. Dadone has not come upon a single battlefield or a single corpse, nor has he seen any trace of a bivouac.

"What can this mean?" he keeps saying in his anguish.

On the eighth day the army enters a mountain pass. On the heights above stands a silken tent, shining in the sun. An awesome silence reigns in these mountains. The army pushes on. . . .

At the bottom of a narrow gorge the Tsar comes upon the remains of his two armies.

The Tsar races up the hill toward the tent. Oh, what a sight! His two sons, bareheaded, lie upon the grass, pierced by their own swords. Their horses roam over the blood-soaked plain.

"Oh, my sons, my sons!" Dadone moans. "Woe is me! Our two heroes, our two falcons have fallen into a trap! I shall die!"

The army joins in his lamentations. Nature herself seems to shake with grief, and the mountains echo their pain.

Suddenly a young girl, as rosy as the dawn, the Princess of Chamakhan, appears before the Tsar, who is struck dumb, like a bird of night surprised by the sun. He stares fixedly at the radiant young maid. He forgets that his sons are dead. She smiles, greets him, and leads him by the hand to her tent. Inside, she prays him to be seated at a table laden with a variety of dishes. Then she leads him to a couch covered with animal skins, where he lies down to rest.

Bewitched by the charms of the Princess of Chamakhan, the Tsar remained with her and regaled himself for a week.

At last he set out for his capital. The Princess followed him. The people were already talking about the

return of their sovereign. Many things, some false, some true, were said about his coming.

As he passed within the ramparts of his city, Dadone was welcomed by loud cheers. People hung onto his chariot and that of the Princess. Suddenly he noticed in the crowd his old friend the eunuch, wearing a white hat from Saratchine.

"I salute you, my father," Dadone said to him. "What can I do for you?"

"All-powerful Tsar, the time has come for us to settle our accounts. Do you remember? In gratitude for my services, you promised to grant me my most cherished wish as though it were your own . . . and so, give me the Princess of Chamakhan!"

"What!" the Tsar cried in astonishment. "Has the devil taken possession of you, or have you lost your mind?

Yes, I made a promise to you, but there are limits to everything. Why do you want this young girl? Do you realize who I am? Tell me what you would prefer . . . the title of boyar? A treasure? A horse from my stables? Half my kingdom?"

"I want only the Princess of Chamakhan!"

Dadone spat in fury and shouted:

"You'll have nothing! Truly, you are your own worst enemy! Now be off while you're still alive! Guards, take him away."

The eunuch wanted to protest, but he realized that you can't argue with some people. The Tsar brandished his scepter and struck him on the forehead. He fell down dead. The people were very frightened. As for the Princess, she broke into peals of laughter, which proved she wasn't afraid of anything.

The procession was about to enter the capital when a sound, soft as velvet, was heard. The cockerel had left his weather vane. With a flutter of wings, he landed on Dadone's head, which he split open with one huge peck. Dadone sighed and died. The Princess of Chamakhan vanished as if she had never existed. This is only a tale, but it will be instructive to good people.

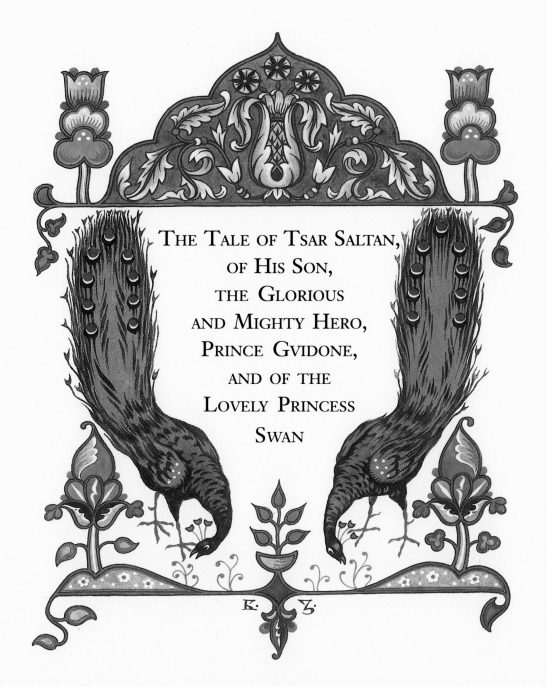

THE TALE OF TSAR SALTAN,
OF HIS SON,
THE GLORIOUS
AND MIGHTY HERO,
PRINCE GVIDONE,
AND OF THE
LOVELY PRINCESS
SWAN

One evening, as shadows fell, three young maidens sat by a window, spinning.

"If I were Tsarina," said one, "I would prepare a huge feast for all the peoples of the earth."

"And if I were Tsarina," said the second sister, "I would weave a piece of linen cloth for all the peoples of the earth."

The third sister declared:

"If I were Tsarina, I would give our father the Tsar a son who would be a hero."

No sooner had she uttered these words than the door quietly opened and the Tsar Saltan, ruler of this land, stepped into the room. Hidden behind a hedge in the garden, he had overheard their conversation. The words spoken by the third maiden had enchanted him.

"Lovely maiden, I salute you," he said. "Come be my Tsarina and present me, at the end of September, with a son who will be a hero! And as for you, dear little sisters, come leave this house and follow us. One of you shall be our seamstress, and the other our pastry cook."

They passed through the hall, went out the front door, and wended their way to the palace.

The Tsar was anything but squeamish. That very evening he married the maiden he had brought to his palace. You can't imagine how they feasted!

At the proper moment the guests led the newlyweds to their ivory bed and left them alone.

In the kitchen the maiden chosen to be the pastry cook is in a boiling fury!

In the tower the maiden chosen to be the seamstress is in a towering rage!

Both are frightfully jealous of the new Tsarina, who in the meantime is keeping her promise by conceiving a child.

A war was in progress, so the Tsar Saltan climbed on his best horse and bade his bride farewell. He made her promise to think of him, but not too much.

Far from home, the Tsar fights fiercely and without respite. The time has come for the Tsarina to give birth to their child.

God gave them a son, twenty-seven inches long.

As the mother eagle watches over the eaglet, so the Tsarina watched over her son. She had at once sent a messenger to her husband, bearing the wonderful news.

But the Seamstress, the Pastry Cook, and their elderly relative Babarika have decided to bring about the downfall of Saltan's bride. They have the messenger thrown into a dungeon and replace him with another, who carries this letter:

> The Tsarina has just given birth. It is
> neither a boy nor a girl, nor a mouse,
> nor a frog, but some unknown animal.

Upon reading these words, Saltan became so furious that he thought of hanging the messenger. However, he thought it over some more, and merely said:
"When I return, I shall make a decision."
Bearing this reply, the messenger gallops off.

He arrives at the palace. The Seamstress, the Pastry Cook, and Babarika have resolved to steal the letter which

42

has been entrusted to the messenger. They get him drunk and slip another letter into his pouch. Thus the poor man delivers to the proper authorities the following decree:

> The Tsar commands his boyars and noblemen to throw the Tsarina and the newborn into the watery deep.

The die was cast. Bemoaning the evil fortune that had befallen their sovereigns, the boyars crowded into the Tsarina's chamber. One of them read aloud the decree concerning the poor young woman.

The Tsarina and her infant son were sealed up inside a barrel, which was then rolled down to the sea.

"The Tsar Saltan so wills it!" shouted the boyars.

Stars shine in the blue heavens. Waves prance over the blue seas.

A cloud floats in the sky. A barrel floats on the sea.

Like a despairing widow, the Tsarina weeps. And her child grows and grows, not day by day, but hour by hour. And her child speaks to the waters:

"Waves, waves! You are free and joyous. You prance about as you please. You polish the sea pebbles. You lap the shore. You carry boats. Do not abandon us. Lead us to land."

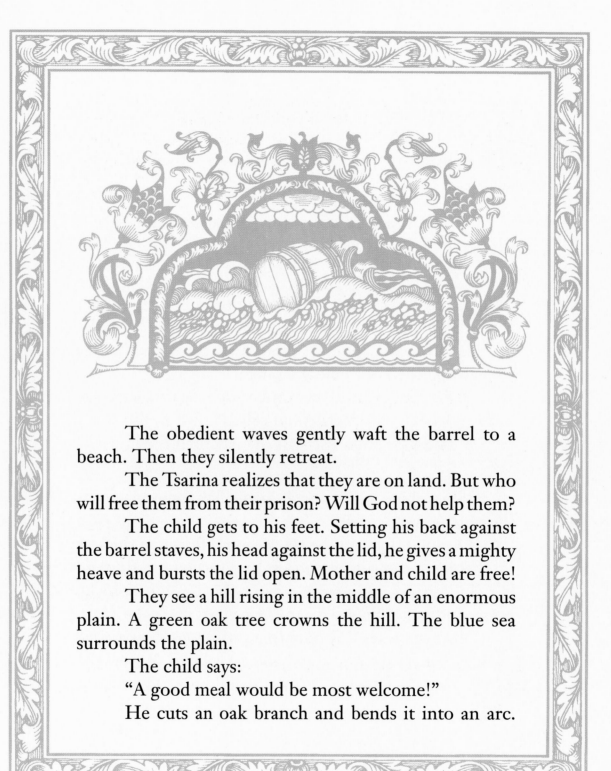

The obedient waves gently waft the barrel to a beach. Then they silently retreat.

The Tsarina realizes that they are on land. But who will free them from their prison? Will God not help them?

The child gets to his feet. Setting his back against the barrel staves, his head against the lid, he gives a mighty heave and bursts the lid open. Mother and child are free!

They see a hill rising in the middle of an enormous plain. A green oak tree crowns the hill. The blue sea surrounds the plain.

The child says:

"A good meal would be most welcome!"

He cuts an oak branch and bends it into an arc.

Then he takes the silken cord from which is hung the cross he wears around his neck, and stretches it between his bow tips. He takes a smaller branch and fashions an arrow. This done, he sets off across the fields in search of game.

He has just reached the seashore when he hears a moan. He looks all about him. He sees a swan struggling in the water. A shrike swoops down toward her. The swan beats her wings as she tries to escape. The bird of prey has already spread his talons and opened his bloodied beak. But the Prince's arrow comes whistling through the air, to strike the bird in the throat. The blood of the shrike spurts upon the waves. The Prince lowers his bow. The shrike falls into the sea, screaming cries that are not the cries of a bird.

The swan swims around her fearsome attacker. She pecks at him viciously. With a great beating of her wings, she drowns the bird of prey. When this is done, she speaks to the Prince in his own tongue:

"You are my savior, my mighty champion. Do not fret if, through my fault, you have nothing to eat for days because your arrow is lost in the sea. A minor mishap! Soon I shall show you my gratitude. You have saved not a swan, but a young maiden. You have killed not a shrike but a sorcerer. I shall never forget it, and you shall always find me. Now go and rest. Go in peace."

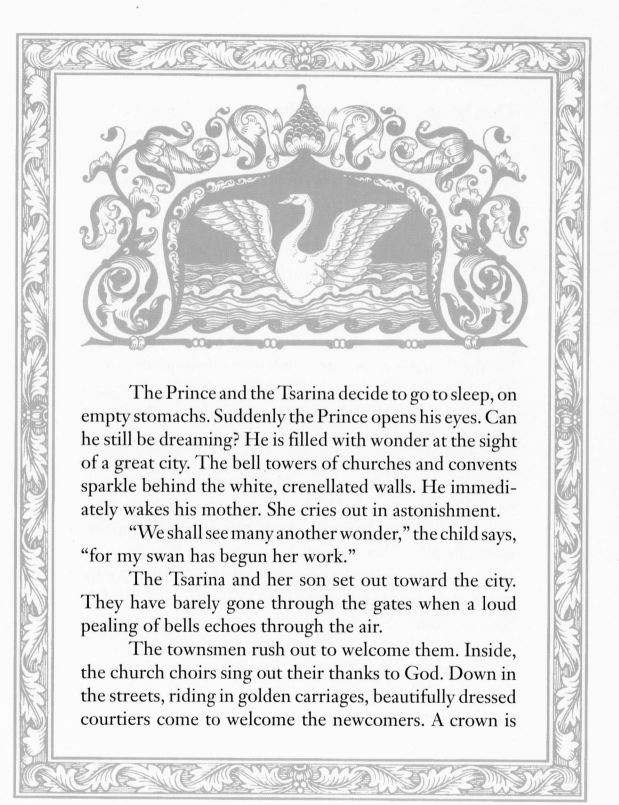

The Prince and the Tsarina decide to go to sleep, on empty stomachs. Suddenly the Prince opens his eyes. Can he still be dreaming? He is filled with wonder at the sight of a great city. The bell towers of churches and convents sparkle behind the white, crenellated walls. He immediately wakes his mother. She cries out in astonishment.

"We shall see many another wonder," the child says, "for my swan has begun her work."

The Tsarina and her son set out toward the city. They have barely gone through the gates when a loud pealing of bells echoes through the air.

The townsmen rush out to welcome them. Inside, the church choirs sing out their thanks to God. Down in the streets, riding in golden carriages, beautifully dressed courtiers come to welcome the newcomers. A crown is

placed on the Prince's head, and he is proclaimed ruler of the land.

With his mother's consent, the Prince enters his palace and that very day begins to reign under the name of Gvidone.

The wind blows over the sea, pushing before it a ship, which slices through the waves, all sails drawing. Up on deck the sailors cannot believe their eyes. A miracle has taken place on this island that they know so well. A city bristling with golden cupolas rises before them. A harbor, protected by a seawall, has been built.

Cannons boom. The ship is invited to enter port, and the passengers debark upon the seawall. Prince Gvidone receives them, offers them food and drink, and asks them:

"What do you trade in, honored guests? Toward what land do you sail?"

One of the travelers replies:

"We have wandered across this vast earth. We have traded fox furs and sables. But we have not yet come to the end of our travels, for we are heading east, toward the kingdom of the illustrious Tsar Saltan, whose realm lies opposite the Isle of Bourian."

"I wish you a happy voyage to the land of the illustrious Tsar Saltan," answers the Prince, "and pray you to convey to him my greetings."

The ship sails off into the distance. Gvidone watches with melancholy as it nears the horizon.

Suddenly he sees the white swan floating on the blue seas.

"Good day, handsome Prince," the bird sings out. "Why are you as sad as an autumn morning?"

"I am gnawed by anxiety," Gvidone replies. "A strange nostalgia has invaded my soul. I wish to see my father."

"Is that all?" exclaims the swan. "Listen, do you want to follow that ship, which is about to drop out of sight?"

"Yes."

The swan spreads her wings and strikes a wavelet, which drenches the Prince from head to toe. And lo, Gvidone is transformed into a tiny mosquito! He flies off into the blue between sky and sea. He catches up with the ship, already far offshore. He lands gently on a spar, then slips down into a crack in the deck.

The winds are favorable. The ship bounds over the waves toward the kingdom of the illustrious Tsar Saltan. Before long, the coastline appears on the horizon.

The travelers go ashore and walk to the palace, where the Tsar awaits them. The little mosquito follows them. And what does he see at last? Saltan, seated upon his throne, dressed in resplendent gold-embroidered robes, his crown upon his head.

But the Tsar is sad. The Seamstress, the Pastry Cook, and their elderly relative Babarika are crouched around him, trying to guess his thoughts.

Saltan invites his guests to join him at his table.

"Noble strangers," he says, "how many years has it been since you left your homes? What countries have you crossed? How do people live beyond the seas? Has a miracle taken place somewhere on this earth?"

"We have roamed this vast world," one of the travelers replies. "All goes well on this earth, and we have seen a miracle. It happened on a dreary desert island. One single, lonely tree grew there. Now an immense city rises on that spot, filled with golden-domed churches, gardens, and shops. Prince Gvidone, who rules this city, sends you his greetings."

Astounded, Tsar Saltan says:

"God willing, I shall go to this fabulous island and I shall pass a few days with Prince Gvidone."

But the Seamstress, the Pastry Cook, and their elderly relative Babarika don't want the Tsar Saltan to leave.

"Truly, that was no miracle!" the Pastry Cook exclaims to him, screwing up one eye. "A city by the sea? Now, I'm going to tell you about a real marvel. In a certain forest is a pine tree. In this pine tree lives a squirrel. And this squirrel sings as he munches his hazelnuts, which are no ordinary nuts. Their shells are of gold and their meat is of emeralds. Now, that's what I call a miracle!"

Hearing this, the Tsar is filled with wonder.

Prince Gvidone flies into a rage. He rams his stinger into his aunt's right eye. The Pastry Cook blanches, faints, and wakes up blind in one eye.

The Seamstress, the elderly relative Babarika, and the servants, shouting loudly, all chase after the culprit.

But Gvidone has already escaped out the window. Untroubled, he flies back across the sea to his realm.

One day, as Gvidone is walking along the seashore, looking at the blue of the water, he sees the white swan gently rocking upon a wave.

"Good day, handsome Prince!" the bird sings out. "Why are you as sad as an autumn morning?"

"I am gnawed by anxiety," Gvidone replies. "I wish to see a certain marvel of which I have heard. In a certain forest is a pine tree. In this pine tree lives a squirrel. And this squirrel sings as he munches on his hazelnuts, which are no ordinary nuts. Their shells are of gold and their meat is of emeralds. Now, that is what I call a miracle! And yet it may be only a lie told by men. . . ."

"They are telling the truth," the swan says. "Fret no more, my friend, my soul. As proof of my love, I shall show you this marvel."

Thrilled, the Prince returns to his palace. Imagine his surprise: In the middle of the main courtyard, at the foot of a pine tree, surrounded by his friends, a squirrel is gnawing at a golden hazelnut, extracting its meat, which is of emeralds. The graceful little animal has cracked the shell of the nut to bits and is singing a song that begins:

> "In the garden,
> In the greens . . ."

Astounded, Prince Gvidone says:

"It is the swan again. Thank you, beloved bird. May the Lord make you as happy as you have made me."

He orders a small crystal palace to be built for the squirrel. A sentry is to guard it. Gvidone instructs his secretary to keep a strict accounting of the nutshells found in the little crystal palace.

Thus the Prince reaped the profits, while the squirrel received the honors.

The wind blows over the sea, pushing before it a ship, which slices through the waves, all sails drawing. The ship approaches the island on which the great city stands.

Cannons boom. The ship is invited to enter port, and the passengers debark upon the seawall. Gvidone receives them, plies them with food and drink, and says:

"What do you trade in, honored guests? To what country do you sail?"

"We have wandered across this vast earth. We have traded horses from the Don. But we have not yet come to the end of our travels, for we are heading east, toward the kingdom of the illustrious Tsar Saltan, whose realm lies opposite the Isle of Bourian," one of the travelers replies.

"I wish you a happy voyage to the land of the illustrious Tsar Saltan," answers the Prince, "and pray you to convey to him my greetings."

The travelers bow before Gvidone and leave the palace to regain their ship.

Down by the seaside Gvidone watches the ship grow small in the distance. Not far offshore, the swan is gently rocking on a wave.

"Beautiful bird, my soul yearns to sail away. . . ."

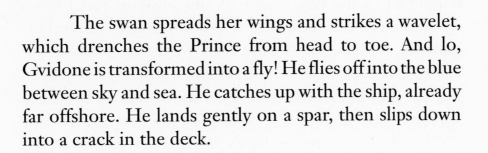

The swan spreads her wings and strikes a wavelet, which drenches the Prince from head to toe. And lo, Gvidone is transformed into a fly! He flies off into the blue between sky and sea. He catches up with the ship, already far offshore. He lands gently on a spar, then slips down into a crack in the deck.

The winds are favorable. The ship bounds over the waves toward the kingdom of the illustrious Tsar Saltan. Before long, the coastline appears on the horizon.

The travelers go ashore and walk to the palace, where the Tsar awaits them. The fly follows them. And what does he see at last? Saltan, seated upon his throne, dressed in resplendent gold-embroidered robes, his crown upon his head.

But the Tsar is sad. The Seamstress, the Pastry Cook, and their elderly relative Babarika are crouched around him, staring at him like ugly, mean toads.

Saltan invites his guests to join him at his table.

"Noble strangers," he says, "how many years has it been since you left your homes? What countries have you crossed? How do people live beyond the seas? Has a miracle taken place somewhere on this earth?"

"We have roamed this vast world," one of the travelers replies. "All goes well on this earth, and we have seen a miracle. It happened on an island. It happened in the city which is the pride of this island, an immense city filled with golden-domed churches, gardens, and shops. A pine tree grows in front of the ruler's palace. A tame squirrel lives in a crystal palace built at the foot of the tree. This squirrel is no ordinary squirrel. He sings as he munches his hazelnuts. And the hazelnuts are no ordinary nuts. Their shells are of gold, and their meat is of emeralds. Servants watch over the squirrel and see to his every need. A secretary keeps a strict accounting of the number of hazelnuts. The army passes constantly in review, in the gentle little beast's honor. The discarded shells are struck into coins and used throughout the world. Women make piles of emeralds deep inside secret caves. Everyone is rich on this island. There are no mean cottages on the island, but palaces wherever you look. Prince Gvidone, who rules this island, sends you his greetings."

"God willing, I shall go to this fabulous island, and I shall pass a few days with Prince Gvidone," announces the astonished Tsar.

But the Seamstress, the Pastry Cook, and their elderly relative Babarika don't want the Tsar Saltan to leave.

"Truly, that is no miracle!" the Seamstress sneers, looking at the Tsar with an evil smile. "A squirrel who shatters nuts with shells of gold and meat of emeralds? True or false, this story has nothing astonishing about it. There is a far greater marvel on this earth: a certain region where every morning the sea washes over a certain deserted beach. As the waters recede, thirty-three huge and handsome warriors, of equal height and dressed in gleaming coats of mail, appear. Their leader is the wise old Tchernomor. That, I assure you, is what I call a miracle!"

The travelers remain silent, not wishing to contradict the Seamstress.

The Tsar marvels over what he has just heard.

Prince Gvidone flies into a rage. He flings himself into his aunt's left eye. The Seamstress blanches and utters a sharp cry: She is blind in one eye! Everybody shouts:

"Squash that fly! Squash it! Just wait . . . just wait!"

But Gvidone has already escaped out the window. Untroubled, he flies back across the sea to his realm.

One day, as Gvidone is walking along the seashore, gazing at the blue of the water, he again sees the white swan, still gently rocking upon a wave.

"Good day, handsome prince!" sings the bird. "Why are you as sad as an autumn morning?"

"I am gnawed by anxiety," Gvidone replies. "I would like to see, right here in my realm, a certain marvel."

"What marvel is that?" asks the swan.

"I would like to see the thirty-three huge and handsome warriors, of equal height and dressed in gleaming coats of mail, who appear on a certain beach when the sea washes over it and then recedes. Their leader is the wise old Tchernomor. . . ."

"Is that all?" says the bird. "I know this marvel well. Fret no more, my friend, my soul. These heroes from the sea are my brothers. Return to your palace and await their coming."

The Prince stands atop his tower. He has forgotten his unhappiness. He looks out to sea. Suddenly the waves begin to churn wildly and to hurl themselves violently against the beach, leaving thirty-three warriors stranded on the sand. Their coats of mail gleam brightly.

Led by a white-haired old man, the heroes march toward the city. Gvidone comes down at once from his tower to greet them. The townspeople rush out to welcome the warriors.

The old man says to the Prince:

"The swan has commanded us to come and watch over your beautiful city. We will mount a guard. Every day we will rise from the deep and stand beneath your ramparts. Thus you shall see us again soon. Now we must return to the sea, for we cannot breathe on land."

The dazzling band of warriors disappears.

The wind blows over the sea, pushing before it a ship, which slices through the waves, all sails drawing. The ship approaches the island on which the great city stands.

Cannons boom. The ship is invited to enter port, and the passengers debark upon the seawall. Prince Gvidone receives them, offers them food and drink, and asks them:

"What do you trade in, honored guests? Toward what land do you sail?"

"We have wandered across this vast earth. We have sold steel from Damascus, silver and gold. But we have not yet come to the end of our travels, for we are heading east, toward the kingdom of the illustrious Tsar Saltan, whose realm lies opposite the Isle of Bourian," one of the travelers replies.

"I wish you a happy voyage to the land of the illustrious Tsar Saltan," answers the Prince, "and pray you to convey to him my greetings."

The travelers bow before Gvidone and leave the palace to regain their ship.

Down by the seaside, Gvidone watches the ship grow small in the distance. Not far offshore, the swan is still gently rocking on a wave.

"Beautiful bird," moans the Prince, "my soul yearns to sail away. . . ."

The swan spreads her wings and strikes a wavelet, which drenches the Prince from head to toe. And lo, Gvidone is transformed into a hornet! He flies off into the blue between sky and sea. He catches up with the ship, already far offshore. He lands gently on a spar, then slips down into a crack in the deck.

The winds are favorable. The ship bounds over the waves toward the kingdom of the illustrious Tsar Saltan. Before long, the coastline appears on the horizon.

The travelers go ashore and walk to the palace, where the Tsar awaits them. The hornet follows them. And what does he see at last? Saltan, seated on his throne, dressed in resplendent gold-embroidered robes, his crown upon his head.

But the Tsar is sad. The Seamstress, the Pastry Cook, and their elderly relative Babarika are crouched around him, watching him with baleful eyes.

Saltan invites his guests to join him at his table.

"Noble strangers," he says, "how many years has it been since you left your homes? What countries have you crossed? How do people live beyond the seas? Has a miracle taken place somewhere on this earth?"

"We have roamed this vast world," one of the travelers replies. "All goes well on this earth, and we have seen a miracle. It happened on an island, where every morning the sea washes over a certain deserted beach. As the waters recede, thirty-three huge and handsome warriors, of equal height and dressed in gleaming coats of mail, appear. Led by the wise old Tchernomor, they mount a guard over the island, whose sovereign, the Prince Gvidone, sends you his greetings."

"God willing, I shall go to this fabulous island and I shall pass a few days with Prince Gvidone," announces the astonished Tsar.

The Seamstress and the Pastry Cook remain silent. Babarika says:

"Truly, that is no miracle! Men who emerge from the sea and mount a guard? True or false, this story has nothing astonishing about it. There is a far greater marvel on this earth. For instance, everyone knows that there lives a princess so lovely that no one ever tires of looking

at her. By day, the brightness of the heavens pales before her beauty. By night, she lights up the earth. A crescent moon shines in her hair. A star sparkles on her forehead. She has the majestic bearing of a peacock. Her voice is like the murmur of a stream. She, I assure you, is what I call a miracle!"

The travelers remain silent, not wishing to contradict such an old woman.

The Tsar marvels over what he has heard. Although extremely cross, Prince Gvidone takes pity on Babarika's eyes. He flits around her, buzzing noisily, lands on her nose, and stings her. A pimple swells up on the old woman's nose.

"Squash that hornet! Squash it! Just wait . . . just wait!"

But Gvidone has already escaped out the window. Untroubled, he flies back across the sea to his realm.

One day, as Gvidone is walking along the seashore, gazing at the blue of the water, he once again sees the white swan, rocking gently as ever upon a wave.

"Good day, handsome Prince!" sings the bird. "Why are you as sad as an autumn morning?"

"I am gnawed by anxiety," Gvidone replies. "All the young men are marrying. I am the only one who remains unwed."

"Are you thinking of any particular maiden?" the swan asks.

"Yes, of a maiden so lovely that no one ever tires of looking at her. By day, the brightness of the heavens pales before her beauty. By night, she lights up the earth. A crescent moon shines in her hair. A star sparkles on her forehead. She has the majestic bearing of a peacock. Her voice is like the murmur of a stream. But does she really exist?"

He anxiously awaits the bird's reply.

The swan is pensive.

"She exists," she suddenly says. "But a bride is not a glove. You cannot simply let her drop from your white hand. Nor can you return her to the sheath that dangles from your belt. Listen . . . I shall give you good advice. Reflect carefully on what I say. It will keep you from going back on your word later."

Taking God as his witness, Gvidone affirms that the time has come for him to marry. He has reflected upon the consequences of marriage. He is prepared to journey to the ends of the earth to find the young princess whose beauty has inflamed his heart.

"Why journey so far?" the swan asks. "Your happiness is close at hand. For I am that princess."

And the swan soars off into the sky. She swoops down toward the shore and settles on top of a bush. She ruffles her feathers and is transformed into a princess! A crescent moon shines in her hair. A star sparkles on her forehead. She is as slender as a peacock. Her voice is as the murmur of a stream.

The Prince embraces the Princess, holds her against his heart, and straightaway leads her to his beloved mother.

Kneeling before the Tsarina, Gvidone says:

"Oh, Mother, I have chosen a bride who will be your dutiful daughter. We ask your blessing, that we may be happy and love each other."

The Tsarina held an icon over their heads.

Weeping, she murmured: "God protect you."

Gvidone married the Princess and lived happily.

The wind blows over the sea, pushing before it a ship, which slices through the waves, all sails drawing. The ship approaches the island on which the great city stands.

Cannons boom. The ship is invited to enter port, and the passengers debark upon the seawall. Prince Gvidone receives them, offers them food and drink, and asks them:

"What do you trade in, honored guests? Toward what land do you sail?"

"We have wandered across this vast earth. We have sold contraband goods. But we have come nearly to the end of our travels, for we are sailing back to our homeland, the kingdom of the illustrious Tsar Saltan."

"I wish you a happy voyage home to the land of the illustrious Tsar Saltan," answers the Prince. "Remind your sovereign that he intended to visit me, and I have waited for him in vain. And convey to him my greetings."

The travelers bow before Gvidone and leave the palace to regain their ship.

This time, not wishing to be separated from his bride, the Prince does not go down to watch them sail away.

The winds are favorable. The ship bounds over the waves toward the kingdom of the illustrious Tsar Saltan. Before long, the coastline appears on the horizon.

The travelers go ashore and walk to the palace, where the Tsar awaits them. And what do they see at last? Saltan, seated upon his throne, dressed in resplendent gold-embroidered robes, a crown upon his head. The Seamstress, the Pastry Cook, and their elderly relative Babarika crouch around him, staring up at him.

Saltan invites his guests to join him at his table.

"Noble strangers," he says, "how many years has it been since you left your homes? What countries have you crossed? How do people live beyond the seas? Has a miracle taken place somewhere on this earth?"

"We have roamed this vast world," one of the travelers replies. "All goes well on this earth, and we have seen a miracle. It happened on an island. It happened in the city which is the pride of this island, an immense city filled with golden-domed churches, gardens, and shops. A pine tree grows in front of the ruler's palace. A tame squirrel lives in a crystal palace built at the foot of the tree.

This squirrel is no ordinary squirrel. He sings as he munches his hazelnuts. And the hazelnuts are no ordinary nuts. Their shells are of gold and their meat is of emeralds. The squirrel is coddled and well looked after. There is another marvel on this island. Every morning the sea washes over a certain deserted beach. As the waters recede, thirty-three huge and handsome warriors, of equal height and dressed in gleaming coats of mail, appear. Led by the wise old Tchernomor, they mount a guard over the island. And the ruler of this island has a wife who is so lovely that no one ever tires of looking at her. By day, the brightness of the heavens pales before her beauty. By night, she lights up the earth. A crescent moon shines in her hair. A star sparkles on her forehead. Prince Gvidone rules this island. All his subjects sing his praises. He asked us to convey to you his greetings and also his displeasure. 'The Tsar Saltan,' he told us, 'intended to pay me a visit. I have awaited him in vain.'"

Saltan can no longer contain his impatience. He orders his fleet to prepare to sail. But the Seamstress, the Pastry Cook, and their elderly relative Babarika do not want him to leave. He will no longer listen to them.

"Who do you think I am?" he growls. "The Tsar— or a child? I shall leave today."

Sitting at a window of his palace, Gvidone gazes out to sea. The sea is calm, with barely a ripple.

Suddenly a fleet appears upon the blue horizon! The mighty fleet of Tsar Saltan looms in the azure distance!

Gvidone rushes out.

"Mother, Mother! And you, my Princess, come quickly! My father has come. . . . "

The ships grow larger. Gvidone has trained his spyglass on them. He catches sight of the Tsar standing on the deck of the finest ship. The Tsar, too, has a spyglass to his eye. The Seamstress, the Pastry Cook, and their elderly relative Babarika stand close to him. They all admire this unknown land.

Cannons boom. Bells peal.

Prince Gvidone goes down to the sea. He greets the Tsar, the Seamstress, the Pastry Cook, and their elderly relative Babarika, and leads them into the city.

The Tsar's retinue arrives before the palace. The Tsar reviews the thirty-three huge and handsome warriors of equal height, who stand at attention with old Tchernomor.

Saltan enters the great courtyard.

Under the slender pine, the squirrel is singing a song. He gnaws upon a golden hazelnut. He removes an emerald and puts it in a bag. The great courtyard is littered with golden shells.

Wide-eyed and open-mouthed in astonishment, Gvidone's guests continue toward the palace. At last they see the Princess. A crescent moon shines in her hair. A star sparkles on her forehead. She has the majestic bearing of a peacock. She walks over to her mother-in-law.

The Tsar looks at his wife and son. He has recognized them! His heart leaps in his bosom.

"What do I see? What! Can it be true?" he stammers.

He is on the verge of fainting. Tears stream down his face. He sweeps the Tsarina, his son, and the young Princess into his arms.

At last they sit down at the table and the feast begins.

The seamstress, the Pastry Cook, and their elderly relative Babarika have fled. They hide.

They are caught. They confess their evil
ways. Weeping, they beg forgiveness.
In celebration of the great day,
the Tsar pardons them and
sends them back to their
homeland. The festiv-
ities end. The Tsar,
half drunk, is
carried to his
room.

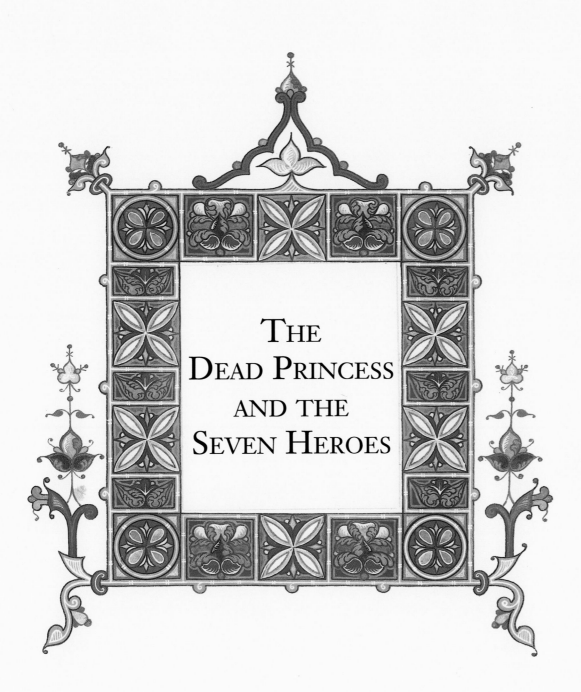

THE
DEAD PRINCESS
AND THE
SEVEN HEROES

The Dead Princess and the Seven Heroes

The Tsar said good-bye to the Tsarina. He was leaving on a very long journey.

And so, seated alone by a window, the Tsarina began the long wait for the Tsar's return.

She stayed by the window from morning to night and never stopped gazing out at the plain.

She stared at it so hard that her eyes hurt. Her beloved friend did not return. All she saw was the snow, which fell in large flakes over the white plain.

Nine months passed. She was still waiting. On Christmas Eve, late at night, the Lord gave her a daughter.

One fine morning the traveler for whom she had waited day and night, the Tsar, arrived at last. She gazed up at him. Completely exhausted, she gave a sorrowful sigh and died.

For a long time the Tsar was unconsolable. But what could he do? After all, he was only a man.

A year went by, as quickly as a fleeting dream. Then the Tsar remarried. Truth to tell, his new bride looked every inch a Tsarina. Tall and slender, with a creamy white complexion, she had remarkable spirit and many rare qualities. Unfortunately, however, she was vain, flighty, and envious.

Among her wedding presents she had found a little talking mirror. Only when she spoke to her mirror was she gentle and gay. She joked and made charming faces. She would say:

"Light of mine eyes, tell me the whole truth. Am I the loveliest, the sweetest, the fairest in all the world?"

"Of course, Tsarina," the mirror would answer. "You are the loveliest, the sweetest, the fairest in all the world."

And the Tsarina would burst into laughter, shrug her shoulders, walk about and snap her fingers. Then, hands on hips, she would pirouette in front of the mirror, admiring her own image.

The daughter of the Tsar was growing up and blossoming forth. Her complexion was as white as snow. Her eyebrows were black. She had a charming nature. Prince Elissei sent an envoy to ask for her hand in marriage. The Tsar gave his consent, and the dowry was agreed upon: seven mill towns and one hundred and forty palaces.

The day before the wedding, as the Tsarina was dressing, she asked her mirror:

"Am I the loveliest, the sweetest, the fairest in all the world?"

"Of course you are beautiful," the mirror replied, "but the loveliest, the sweetest, the fairest in all the world is the Princess."

The Tsarina jumped up, raised her arm, struck the mirror, and stamped her foot.

"You're just a miserable slab of glass!" she screamed. "You lie, simply to vex me. How dare the Tsar's daughter compare herself to me? I'll put her in her place right now. So this is what she has become! No wonder she's so fair: Her mother spent her whole pregnancy gazing out at the snow. Tell me . . . how can she possibly compare with me?

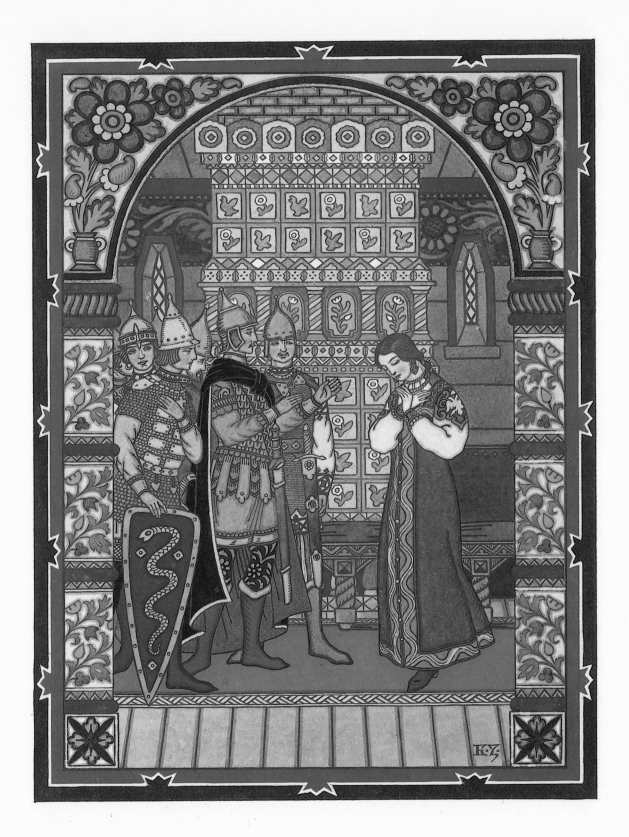

Admit it, I am the loveliest. Search our kingdom, search all the universe, and you will not find a woman like me. Is it not true?"

"Yet," replied the mirror, "the Princess is the loveliest, the sweetest, the fairest of all maidens."

Choking with jealousy, the Tsarina threw the mirror under a stool. She called for her maid, Tcherniavka, and ordered her to take the Princess into the forest, to tie her to a tree, and to leave her there to be eaten by wolves.

The devil himself is powerless against a woman's wrath. There was nothing to be done. Tcherniavka led the Princess into a forest so wild and dense that the poor thing immediately guessed her fate.

"My friend, my life, what have I done?" she pleaded to the maidservant, with terror in her voice. "Don't let me die! I'll show you how grateful I am when I become Tsarina. . . ."

Tcherniavka, who loved the Princess, did not tie her to the tree, but set her free, saying:

"Don't weep, and may the Lord protect you!"

Tcherniavka returned to the palace.

"Where is the young girl?" the Tsarina asked her.

"Alone, deep in the forest," she answered. "She is tied securely to a tree. If the wolves who find her are really fierce, she will not suffer long."

Word was put about that the Princess had disappeared. The Tsar shed many tears. Prince Elissei prayed fervently to God and set out in search of his beloved promised bride.

At dawn the next day, as she was trying to find her way out of the forest, the young Princess came upon a little house. A dog ran at her, barking, but stopped his barking at once, as if he had recognized her. She pushed open the door of the house and found herself in a courtyard. The dog was still following her. He pranced about and licked her hands.

The Princess opened another door, which led her into a bright room with a tiled stove, an oak table, wooden benches covered with rugs, and sacred icons on the walls. The hapless girl realized that this was the home of good people. Here she would be safe. But why was the house empty?

She went through the rest of the house, putting everything in order. She lit a small candle and offered it to God. She also kindled a fire in the stove. Then she lay down to sleep, under the eaves.

It is suppertime. A loud noise echoes in the courtyard. Seven resolute and rosy knights with large mustaches march into the house.

"How marvelous!" exclaims the oldest knight. "How clean, how neat! Who has been at work here while we were away? Come out of hiding and become our friend, O industrious stranger! If you are old, you shall be our uncle! If you are a strapping lad, you shall be our brother! If you are a woman and old, you shall be our mother! If you are a young maiden, you shall be our sister!"

The Princess crawls out of her nook. She curtsies to the seven rosy knights. Blushing, she asks their forgiveness for having entered their house without permission.

The seven knights have taken the young maiden for a Princess. They ask her to sit in the place of honor, under the icons. They offer her a platter of cake and a glass of wine. She refuses the wine but cuts the cake. She is very tired and asks her hosts for permission to go back to sleep.

So the seven knights lead her into a pretty bedroom and leave her to her slumbers.

Time goes by. The Princess is still living in the home of the seven knights. She is anything but bored. In the morning, at break of day, the young men joyously set forth to hunt gray duck. Sometimes they have target practice, or else they practice lopping off the head of a Tartar with one swoop of the sword. At other times they chase through the forest a certain Circassian from Piatigorsk.

Like a good mistress of the house, the Princess never leaves her new home. She sees to everything. She prepares everything. The seven knights approve of all she does. Time goes by.

By now the seven knights are in love with the lovely maiden. One day at dawn they come into her room. Bowing, the oldest says:

"As you know, lovely maiden, you are our sister. We are seven, and we love you. Each of us would be happy to marry you, but that is impossible! In the name of the Lord, choose. Be the bride of one of us! Be a gracious sister to the rest of us! Why do you shake your head? Why do you refuse? Do the wares displease the merchant?"

"Handsome knights," she replies, "my brothers, may God strike me down if I lie! I cannot listen to you! I am betrothed! I cannot choose among you. In my eyes, you are all brave, all charming. I love you all. But I have given myself forever to another. I belong to Prince Elissei, who is dearer to me than anything else in the world."

The seven knights are silent. They scratch their heads in embarrassment. The oldest, still bowing, says:

"To express a longing is no sin. Given the situation, I shall not bring this up again."

"I am grateful for your delicacy," the Princess answers softly. "I cannot accept your offer, but please don't hold it against me."

The seven knights leave the room in silence. Harmony reigns, as before, in the little house.

The mean Tsarina was still thinking about the Princess. She could not forgive her. She also held a grudge against her mirror and often hurled insults at it. But finally she decided that she wanted to consult it again. She went to find it. Then, putting the mirror before her face, she said with a smile:

"Little mirror, I salute you! Tell me the truth. Am I the loveliest, the sweetest, the fairest in all the world?"

"Of course you are beautiful," replied the mirror, "but the one who lives, forgotten, in the green forest, in the home of the seven knights, is still more beautiful than you."

The Tsarina flew into a rage at Tcherniavka:

"You dared to betray me? Tell me all!"

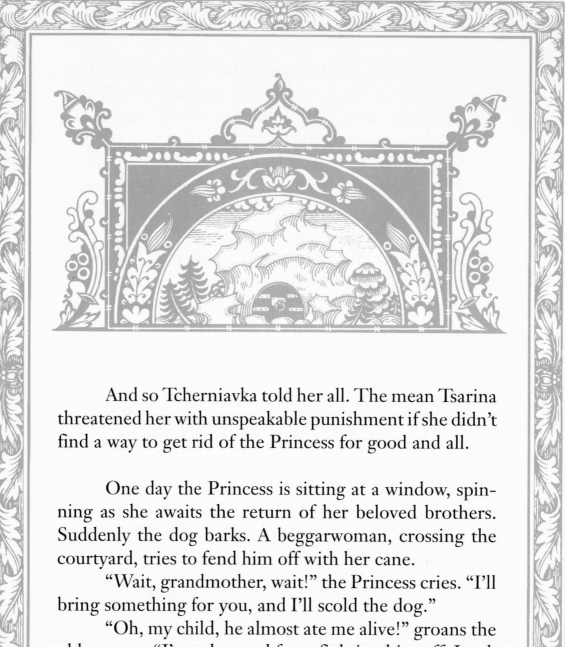

And so Tcherniavka told her all. The mean Tsarina threatened her with unspeakable punishment if she didn't find a way to get rid of the Princess for good and all.

One day the Princess is sitting at a window, spinning as she awaits the return of her beloved brothers. Suddenly the dog barks. A beggarwoman, crossing the courtyard, tries to fend him off with her cane.

"Wait, grandmother, wait!" the Princess cries. "I'll bring something for you, and I'll scold the dog."

"Oh, my child, he almost ate me alive!" groans the old woman. "I'm exhausted from fighting him off. Look at him! He's going to attack me again! Come quickly!"

The maiden hurries toward her, but as soon as she crosses the threshold, the dog springs at her, preventing her from going farther.

The beggarwoman tries to approach the Princess. The dog, ferocious now, stops her in her tracks.

"How strange!" the maiden says. "He must have slept badly."

She throws a loaf of bread to the old woman, saying: "Catch!"

"I thank you," the beggarwoman says. "May God bless you! Pray, would you accept this?"

She throws a golden apple to the Princess. The dog howls.

The Princess turns the apple over several times in her hand.

"You can eat it when you have nothing better to do, my beauty," the old woman cries. "Thank you for giving me bread."

She disappears.

The dog gazes mournfully up at the young maiden. He whines. He is trying to say: "Throw that apple away! Quickly—throw it away!"

She pats the dog tenderly. "Come, Sokolka," she says. "Lie down." And she returns to her room to await her brothers. She sits down at her loom.

Often she glances at the apple, which she has put down beside her. The fruit looks plump and juicy. It is so

golden, so fragrant! You can even see the pips, for the skin is as transparent as a butterfly's wing.

The Princess does not want to eat the apple before supper. But she can't resist! She raises it to her lips and takes a bite.

She falls down, lifeless. The apple rolls to the other side of the room.

Her head rests on the bench beneath the icons. The maiden appears to be dead.

The seven knights are on their way home from a marvelous outing when they see the little dog running toward them, barking loudly.

"It's a bad omen," they think. "Something dreadful has happened."

Up in her room, how they weep and wail! The dog pounces on the apple, eats it, and falls dead.

The seven knights gather sadly around the dead Princess. They recite a prayer and then lift their sister up and begin to dress her for burial. Suddenly they change their minds. Her face is so calm. She looks so sweet in the protective arms of sleep. But she is not breathing.

They wait for three days. She does not awaken. And so they decide to put the Princess in a crystal coffin. They carry it on their shoulders at midnight to the top of a mountain and set it down there.

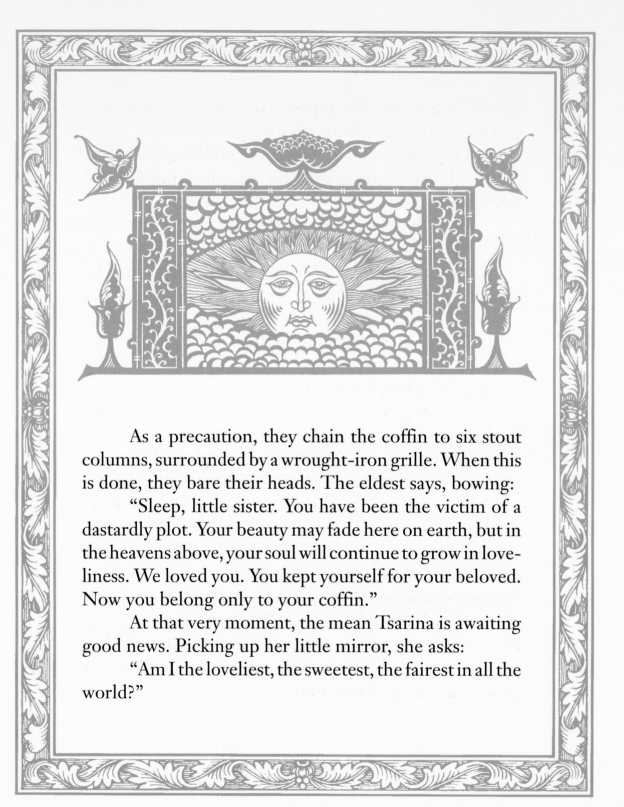

As a precaution, they chain the coffin to six stout columns, surrounded by a wrought-iron grille. When this is done, they bare their heads. The eldest says, bowing:

"Sleep, little sister. You have been the victim of a dastardly plot. Your beauty may fade here on earth, but in the heavens above, your soul will continue to grow in loveliness. We loved you. You kept yourself for your beloved. Now you belong only to your coffin."

At that very moment, the mean Tsarina is awaiting good news. Picking up her little mirror, she asks:

"Am I the loveliest, the sweetest, the fairest in all the world?"

"Yes," answers the mirror, "you are the loveliest, the sweetest, the fairest in all the world."

Prince Elissei rides in search of his intended bride. He does not find her. He weeps. He questions the passersby. Some people find his rather discombobulated questions a bit strange. A few laugh at him. Some turn their backs on him.

Finally he addresses the sun:

"O sun," he exclaims, "you who travel through the sky, you who make spring follow winter, you who see us all, will you answer me? Will you tell me you have seen the Princess whom I seek? I am her betrothed."

"Little friend," replies the red sun, "I have not seen the Princess whom you seek. Perhaps she is dead. Perhaps the dead moon, my neighbor, has seen her. . . ."

Elissei waits for night. At last the moon rises in the sky.

"My friend, the moon," he calls out, "companion of the stars, can you answer me? I am looking for my betrothed. Have you seen her?"

"My brother," the bright moon answers, "I have not seen her. Anyway, I am not always in the sky. Perhaps your betrothed is so pale that I cannot see her. . . . "

"Woe is me!" the Prince murmurs.

The moon speaks again.

"Ask the wind. Who knows? He will answer you. Have courage. . . . Farewell!"

Elissei cries to the wind:

"You who are strong, you who can tame the clouds and roil the sea, you who fear only God . . . speak to me! Have you seen the Princess I love? I am her betrothed."

"Listen," the wind replies. "Yonder, beyond that melodious stream, you will find a mountain. Inside that mountain there is a dark cave. Inside that cave there is a crystal coffin, surrounded by columns and chained to them. Inside that coffin lies your betrothed."

The wind has blown away. The Prince rides off, weeping.

He looks for the mountain that the wind described. He catches sight of it. He hurries toward it. He comes to the mouth of the cave. His courage fails him, but he soon takes heart.

He makes his way through the gloom of the dark cave. All of a sudden he can make out the shape of the crystal coffin, the radiant face of the Princess!

He strikes the coffin with all his might and shatters it. The maiden awakens. She looks around her, astonished.

"I have slept a long time," she sighs.

She sits up and steps out of the coffin.

They embrace, weeping.

Elissei sweeps up his beloved in his arms and carries her into the light. What do you suppose they say to each other?

The good news spreads like wildfire:

"The daughter of the Tsar is not dead!"

The mean Tsarina sits before her mirror and repeats:

"Am I the loveliest, the sweetest, the fairest in all the world?"

"Of course you are beautiful," the mirror replies, "but the Princess is still more beautiful than you."

She breaks the mirror, throws it on the rug, and rushes toward the door, which has just opened.

She sees the Princess and drops dead of rage.

The wedding of Elissei and the Princess
was celebrated immediately after
the funeral of the dead Tsarina.
It was the greatest feast
ever given in all
the world.

THE TALE
OF THE
GOLDEN FISH

THE TALE OF THE GOLDEN FISH

An old fisherman and his wife had lived rather drearily for thirty-three years in a miserable hovel on the edge of the blue sea. The wife was very old. The old fisherman caught fish. His wife did weaving. One day the man caught nothing but mud in his net. He threw the net back in the water. He caught only seaweed. He threw it again. This time he caught a little fish, an extraordinary fish, a golden fish. And the fish moaned in a human voice:

"Kindly old man, let me return to the sea! In exchange for my liberty, I will give you whatever you want."

The fisherman was astonished. He was also worried. In all the thirty-three years that he had been catching fish, he had never seen one that talked. He threw the fish back into the sea, tenderly saying:

"Be free in the blue sea, and may God protect you! I refuse to be paid a ransom!"

He returned to his hut and recounted his adventure to his wife:

"Today I caught an extraordinary fish, a golden fish. He could talk, just like you and me. He asked me to throw him back into the sea, his home. In return, he offered me whatever I wanted. I didn't dare accept. I threw him back into the water."

His wife began to hurl insults at him:

"Imbecile, simpleton, who wouldn't accept such an offer? You could at least have asked him for a new bucket! Ours is cracked."

The fisherman went down to the blue sea and stood by its turbid waves. He called to the little golden fish. The fish swam up to him and asked:

"What do you want, kindly old man?"

Bowing low, he answered:

"Forgive me, my lord fish! My wife reproached me. She shows no pity for my age. She wants a new bucket, for ours is cracked."

"Don't worry," the fish replied, "and may the Lord keep you. You shall have your new bucket."

The fisherman returned to his hut and found his wife standing beside a brand-new bucket. She began to heap even more insults upon him:

"Imbecile, simpleton, do you call a new bucket a present? Go find the little fish and ask for a cottage."

The fisherman again went down to the blue sea and stood by its turbid waves. He called to the golden fish. The little fish swam up to him and said:

"What do you want, kindly old man?"

Bowing low, he answered:

"Forgive me, my lord fish! My wife is even more furious with me than before. She shows no pity for my age. The shrew now demands a cottage."

"Don't worry," the fish of gold replied, "and may the Lord keep you. So be it. You shall have a cottage."

The fisherman returned to his miserable hovel.

But not a trace of it remained. Before him was a cottage with a white brick chimney and a door of oak.

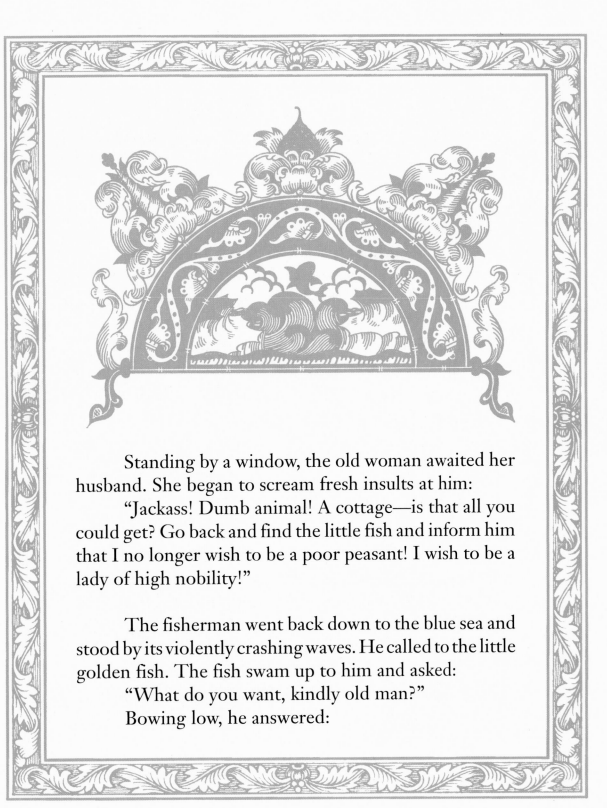

Standing by a window, the old woman awaited her husband. She began to scream fresh insults at him:

"Jackass! Dumb animal! A cottage—is that all you could get? Go back and find the little fish and inform him that I no longer wish to be a poor peasant! I wish to be a lady of high nobility!"

The fisherman went back down to the blue sea and stood by its violently crashing waves. He called to the little golden fish. The fish swam up to him and asked:

"What do you want, kindly old man?"

Bowing low, he answered:

"Forgive me, my lord fish! My wife is crazier than ever. She shows no pity for my age. She no longer wants to be a peasant. She wishes to be a lady of the high nobility."

"Don't worry, and may the Lord keep you!" answered the little fish.

The fisherman returned to his cottage.

And what does he see? His wife, standing on the front steps of a castle. She is wrapped in a sable coat. A gold-embroidered toque sits on her head. She is wearing red mules. She has a pearl necklace around her neck and rings upon her fingers. Crowding about her are many servants, whom she often slaps. She also pulls their hair.

The old man says to her:

"My compliments, lovely lady. I trust you are satisfied?"

She screamed dreadful insults at him and then sent him off to the stables.

One week went by, then another. The unfortunate woman had completely lost her mind. One evening she ordered her husband to go back and find the little fish.

"Tell him that I no longer wish to be a lady of the high nobility. I wish to be queen."

Terrified, the old fisherman tries to reason with her:

"What is this, woman? What magic potion have you drunk? Why, you can't even walk without stumbling,

you can't even speak correctly—and you want to be queen? You'd be the laughingstock of the whole kingdom!"

She slapped him.

"Churl, you dare contradict me? I am asking you politely. . . . Go speak to the little fish, or else my lackeys will drag you there!"

The fisherman went back down to the sea and stood by its tumultuous black waves. He called to the little golden fish. The fish swam up to him and asked:

"What do you want, kindly old man?"

Bowing low, he answered:

"Forgive me, my lord fish! My wife is definitely insane. She wishes to be queen."

"Don't worry, and may the Lord keep you," the fish replied. "So be it. Your wife shall be queen."

The fisherman went off.

And what did he see? A magnificent palace. In one of the stately rooms of the palace, he finds his wife sitting at a table. Boyars serve her platters of delicious foods, while others pour exotic wines. Still others are slicing gingerbread. Behind her stand warriors with halberds at their shoulders.

Terror-stricken, the fisherman says:

"Hail, formidable Majesty! Are you satisfied now?"

Without so much as a glance at him, she commands:

"Guards! Throw him out!"

One of the boyars springs toward him and throws out the poor, flabbergasted old man.

In the courtyard of the palace, armed men threaten to kill him.

The people screech at him:

"You bumpkin! You really asked for it! Let this be a lesson to you! Don't get too big for your britches!"

One week went by, then another. The old queen, in a state of extreme agitation, ordered her flunkeys to fetch her husband.

He arrives.

"Go speak to the little fish," she commands him, "and tell him I no longer wish to be Queen of the Earth. I wish to be Queen of the Waters. I want to live in the

Ocean Sea and have the little fish obey me and run my errands."

The fisherman, not daring to open his mouth, went back down to the now thundering, raging, and roaring blue sea. He called to the little golden fish. The fish swam up to him and asked:

"What do you want, kindly old man?"

Bowing low, he answered:

"Forgive me, my lord fish! What can I do with this accursed woman? She no longer wishes to be Queen of the Earth. She now wishes to reign over the Ocean Sea, so that you'll have to obey her and run her errands."

The little golden fish said not one word. But his tail whipped the waves and he disappeared into the blue sea. Standing by the edge of the sea, the fisherman waited for his answer.

Finally he went off. And what did he see?

His wife sitting on the stoop of
the miserable hovel, beside
the cracked
bucket.